♡Eva and the Lost Pony♡

Read more OWL DIARIES books!

OWL DIARIES

♡ Eva and the Lost Pony ♡

Rebecca
Elliott

BRANCHES

SCHOLASTIC INC.

For Toby, who one day decided that Benjy was his butler and named him "Humbleton." And for Benjy, who was okay with this. xx — R.E.

Library of Congress Cataloging-in-Publication Data
Names: Elliott, Rebecca, author.
Title: Eva and the lost pony / Rebecca Elliott.
Description: First edition. | New York, NY : Branches/Scholastic Inc., 2018. | Series: Owl diaries ; 8 | Summary: Eva decides that warning all the animals in the forest about the approaching storm is a perfect project to prove herself worthy of taking the Owl Oath, but when she stops to help a lost pony and they get caught in the storm, they have to take shelter in a cave, and end up helping each other to stay brave.
Identifiers: LCCN 2017021917| ISBN 9781338163032 (pbk. : alk. paper) | ISBN 9781338163049 (hardcover : alk. paper)
Subjects: LCSH: Owls–Juvenile fiction. | Ponies–Juvenile fiction. | Helping behavior–Juvenile fiction. | Courage–Juvenile fiction. | Friendship–Juvenile fiction. | CYAC: Owls–Fiction. | Ponies–Fiction. | Helpfulness–Fiction. | Courage–Fiction. | Friendship–Fiction.
Classification: LCC PZ7.E45812 En 2018 | DDC [Fic]–dc23
LC record available at https://lccn.loc.gov/2017021917

ISBN 978-1-338-16304-9 (hardcover) / ISBN 978-1-338-16303-2 (paperback)

10 9 8 7 6 5 4 3 2 1   18 19 20 21 22

Printed in China   38
First edition, March 2018

Book design by Marissa Asuncion
Edited by Katie Carella

♡ Table of Contents ♡

My Tree House

11

9

Woodpine Avenue

♡ Remember Me? ♡

Sunday

Hello Diary,
 It's Eva Wingdale here! Are you ready for another **FLAPERRIFIC** adventure? First, let me tell you a bit about myself...

<u>I love</u>:

Parties

Pets

The word <u>moon</u>

Dad's jokes

What do you call a cow playing a guitar?

A <u>MOO</u>sician!

The sound of rain

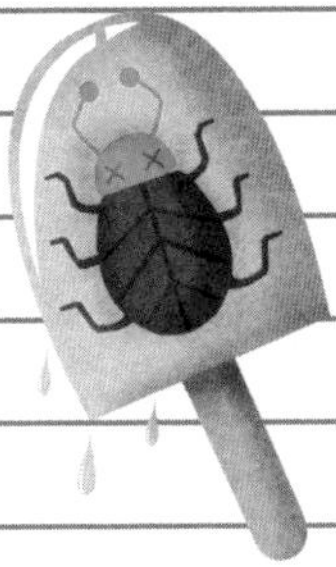

Mom's
bugsicles

Baxter's
costumes

Styling my
feathers

<u>I DO NOT love</u>:

Flying in the rain

Mom's cockroach chowder

The word y<u>a</u>wn

Being picked last for the wingball team

Taking medicine

Sitting still

Wasp stings

Gloopy mud

My family is **WING-TASTIC!**

Here is a picture of us on Egg Day:

Mom

Dad

Baby Mo

Me

Humphrey

This is Baxter – my lovely little pet bat.

Being an owl is **WING-CREDIBLE!**

We learn to fly when we're only a few weeks old.

We're awake all through the night.

We're asleep all through the day.

And we have HUGE eyes that see in the dark!

We also live in cool tree houses.

My family lives next door to Lucy Beakman's family.

My Tree House

11

9

Lucy is my best friend in the whole **OWLIVERSE**.

We both go to school at Treetop
Owlementary, and this is our class photo.

That reminds me I have school
tomorrow. I'd better get to sleep. Good
day, Diary!

♡ The Owl Oath ♡

Monday

At school today, Mrs. Featherbottom hooted something super important.

Owlets! This is a very special week. It is time for you to take your Owl Oath.

We had heard of the Owl Oath, but we wanted to know more so we listened carefully.

All animals of the forest have a duty to protect one another. But owls are known as the **Keepers of the Forest**, so we take this duty very seriously. The Owl Oath is our promise to always be wise and brave and kind to the other forest folk.

Everyone was excited to hear more.

Before you take the Owl Oath, you each need to do something that shows you understand the true meaning of the oath. You can create a painting, a poem, a dance, or do something nice for another animal. You will share your project with the class on Friday. Then on Saturday, you will take the oath at a special ceremony before the **Keepers of the Forest** Ball.

Yay!

Mrs. Featherbottom handed out
copies of the oath so we could learn it.

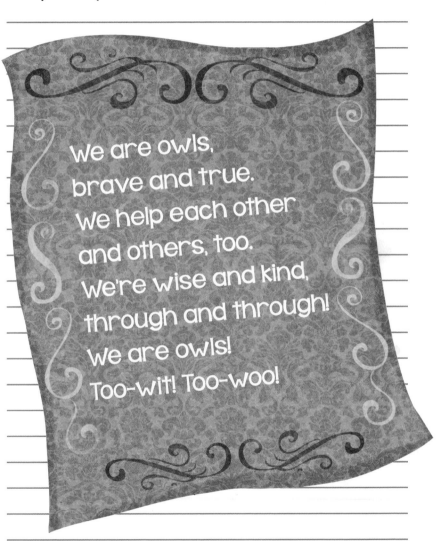

We are owls,
brave and true.
We help each other
and others, too.
We're wise and kind,
through and through!
We are owls!
Too-wit! Too-woo!

At lunch, my friends and I couldn't stop **HOOTING** about the oath, the ceremony, and the ball.

I can't believe it's Owl Oath week!

I'm so excited!

We need to come up with the perfect projects!

Should we meet up after school to brainstorm ideas?

Yes! We can also practice the oath!

Sue flew over to our table.

After school, Lucy, Hailey, and I dressed up our pets as different forest creatures.

Baxter   Rex   Chester

Then we helped them — just like the Owl Oath tells us to do!

Next, we practiced the oath. But we kept getting it wrong. It was so funny!

Then we talked about the projects. Lucy AND Hailey had **EGG-CELLENT** ideas already.

I'm going to draw an owl with her wings around all the other forest creatures.

I'm going to write a story about a brave owl who stops a forest fire.

Wow. Those are great ideas!

I tried to come up with ideas for my project, but I couldn't think of ANYTHING good.

Oh, Diary. What am I going to do?

The Storm Soldier

On the way to school, Lucy and I saw dark clouds in the sky.

My mom says there's a big storm coming!

I love the sound of rain! But storms can be scary.

Everyone in class was talking about the storm.

Then everyone started talking about their projects.

Everyone's ideas were great. But I still didn't know what to do!

After school, the clouds were darker. I saw lots of animals rushing to get home. I guess they were worried the storm might come early.

Suddenly, I had a **FLAP-TASTIC** idea for my project:

I will become a Storm Soldier. I'll fly around the forest making sure everyone is prepared for the big storm!

I made a to-do list:

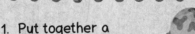

1. Put together a Storm Soldier outfit

2. Make posters that give tips on how to:

   - Storm-proof your home

   - Stay safe during the storm

3. Put the posters up around the forest

I put together my Storm Soldier outfit.

I told my family about my project.

I love it, Eva!

Watch out, storm! Here comes the Storm Soldier!

I started making posters right away.

What do you think, Diary?

STORM ALERT!
- Stay Safe
- Stay inside
- Put Leaves and twigs outside your house to make it stronger

I hope my project will show that I am ready to take the Owl Oath. Now this Storm Soldier needs her sleep. Good day, Diary!

♡ Thunder Disaster! ♡

I woke up super early and put up my posters.

At school, I told my friends about my Storm Soldier project.

That's great, Eva!

Your project will <u>really</u> help others!

I had planned to put up more posters after school. But just as we were about to head home —

DISASTER!

The storm came early! The thunder was super LOUD. The lightning was super BRIGHT. And it was raining super HARD.

The storm is bad. We're all going to have to stay here.

You mean we have to <u>sleep</u> here?

That's right, class. I'll get blankets. We can all huddle up together.

When everyone
fell asleep, I looked
out at the storm.
I hoped the other
forest creatures
were okay and that
my posters had
helped some of
them.

Mrs. Featherbottom woke us up in the middle of the day. I thought it would be bright and sunny outside, but the clouds were still dark.

Class, the storm has stopped. You should all fly home as fast as you can! I'm worried the storm could start up again.

I was flying home super fast when I saw a pony. He looked lost!

I thought about the Owl Oath.

And I remembered that I'm the Storm Soldier . . .

The clouds were getting darker as I flew down to see if the pony was okay.

Hi. I'm Eva.

Humbleton trotted after me, but then the storm started up again.

The wind was so strong I struggled to fly. Then a tree blew down right in front of us!

We stayed in the cave for the rest of the day.

I felt really scared while the rain poured and the winds howled.

But my new friend helped me feel less scared. He talked to me gently.

Thank you again for flying down to help me. Why did you?

I wanted to help. And I'm taking the Owl Oath on Saturday.

I've heard that's very important.

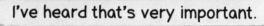

It is. And I became a Storm Solider to show I know the true meaning of the oath. I wanted to help other animals prepare for the storm. I hung up posters to help them. But the storm came early, and I'm sure my posters all blew away. So I didn't really help anyone.

You helped me. I'd be scared all alone.

I thought about the time Baxter went missing and how worried I was about him. I didn't want my parents to have to worry about me like that.

Will this storm ever end??

♡ A Big Sorry ♡

Thursday

At last, the storm was over! Now we had to find our way home. It was dark outside so I could see really well! But Humbleton couldn't see much at all. (Ponies are not as good at seeing in the dark as owls are.)

Don't worry. I'll guide you through the fallen trees.

Thanks, Storm Soldier!

44

Finally, we reached my tree house.

Thank goodness you're safe, Eva!

My family and I helped Humbleton get back home.

Thanks, Eva! Good-bye!

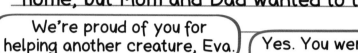

I wanted to go to bed when we got home, but Mom and Dad wanted to talk.

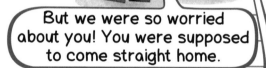

We're proud of you for helping another creature, Eva.

Yes. You were very brave and very kind.

But we were so worried about you! You were supposed to come straight home.

Next time, you **must** ask us before you go flying off on your own. That storm was dangerous!

I'm sorry. I'll never do something like this ever again.

Mom scooted me into bed.

Oh, Diary, what will I say about my project in class tomorrow?

♡ I'm No Owl! ♡

Hi Diary,

On the way to school, I told Lucy everything that had happened with Humbleton.

Wow, Eva! That sounds exciting!

Yes, but my posters didn't help Humbleton stay safe in the storm.

But YOU helped Humbleton.

Maybe. But he helped _me_ more.

There wasn't anything Lucy could say to make me feel better.

Soon, it was time to share our projects.

I slumped down in my chair, hoping Mrs. Featherbottom wouldn't call on me. My project stinks — it didn't work. I have <u>nothing</u> to share with my class!

My classmates' projects were all **OWLMAZING**.

Zara's selfies:
Forest Friends

Sue's dress:
Animals United

Zac's cartoon:
Super Owl to the Rescue!

Yo, you know I'm an owl,
And that I hoot, I don't growl!
I'm in the trees with the bees
I don't live underground.
And if you need a feathered friend
To protect and to defend,
Then I'll be brave, wise, and true,
'Cause I'm a funky forest dude.

Carlos's rap:
"The Funky Forest Dude"

Lucy's picture:
Hugging Wings

Crash! Crackle! A burnt smell filled the air! The little brown and orange owl leapt out of bed. With no time to waste she flew into the kitchen to get water to put out the forest fire. But she found her dad cooking breakfast. He'd burned the toast again!

"There's no forest fire?" she said.

"No," said her dad, smiling, "but it's good to know there are owls as brave as you around if there was ever a fire!"

Kiera's story:
"The Forest Fire"

Alone in the woods.
Who will save you when in need?
Hoo will? Owls! That's hoo!

Hailey's poem:
"Who? Hoo! Hoo!"

Macy's cake:
Tree of Love

George's model:
The Brave Owl King

I'm a believer in the beaver,
I'm in tune with the raccoon.
I like to share with the bear
And the hare and the baboon.
I will be there if you need me,
Be you mouse or grouse or deer,
'Cause I'm brave, wise, and true
And owl always be right here.

Jacob's song:
"Owl Always Be Here"

Lily's dance:
A Woodland Heart

Everyone looked at me. It was my turn.

My cheeks went red as I flew to the front of the class. I held up one of my posters with shaking wings.

My project was to become the Storm Soldier to help other animals prepare for the storm. I put up posters, but I think they blew down. And I know animals still got lost. Like a pony I found. I tried to be brave and wise but . . . I was scared. The pony kept ME calm. He helped me more than I helped him. And I hadn't told my family where I was going, which was not a smart thing to do . . . They got upset. So really, my project didn't <u>help</u> anyone.

Mrs. Featherbottom flew over to me.

Eva, it's okay. You tried to be helpful. Things don't always go as planned or turn out the way we hope they will.

I don't think I'm ready to take the Owl Oath, Mrs. Featherbottom.

I think you are. But you need to believe it yourself. If you think about how <u>kind</u> you were trying to be, you'll know that you're ready to become a true **Keeper of the Forest**.

After school, Lucy and Hailey tried to cheer me up. They put on a fashion show of their outfits for tomorrow's ball.

Come on, Eva! Try on your outfit!

There's no point. I'm not going.

You have to come, Eva! You're totally ready to take the oath.

Thanks, but I just don't feel ready.

I had just gotten into bed when my brother Humphrey stormed in.

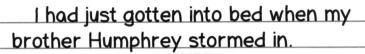

> I can't believe you didn't tell us where you were going the other night.

> I know, Humphrey! I told Mom and Dad I'm sorry!

> But I was . . . well, I was worried, too, okay?

> You're right. I'm sorry, Humphrey.

> Anyhoo, I took the oath. So, YOU should totally take it. Oh, but take a bath first because you smell bad.

> Oh, Humphrey. Go away!

Diary, should I take the oath tomorrow? My friends and family seem to believe in me, but I'm not sure that I do.

♡ A Surprise Visitor ♡

Saturday

Lucy called me on her **PINEPHONE** first thing tonight.

Hey, Eva! Are you ready to take the oath today?

I still don't feel brave or wise enough to take it.

But you <u>have</u> to take it!

I'll think about it. Okay?

I put on my outfit for the ball, just in case I decided to go.

Then Humphrey barged into my room again.

I didn't know who it could be.

I opened the door and . . .

ALL of my classmates were outside my tree house! Mrs. Featherbottom and Principal Eggmington were there!

There were lots of other animals, too!

Diary, guess who turned up next!

Humbleton!

Hi, Eva! You were so <u>brave</u> and <u>kind</u> to fly down to help me during the storm. And you were definitely <u>wise</u> when you found that cave for us to shelter in. I'd probably still be lost if it weren't for you. So thank you!

You're welcome, Humbleton. Thank YOU for being such a good friend when I got scared.

Anytime. Now, Eva, if anyone's ready to take the owl oath, it's you! Go for it!

You know, I think I <u>will</u>!

I can't wait to take the oath, Diary! I'll tell you all about it tomorrow!

The **Keepers of the Forest** Ball

Sunday

Hi Diary,
    Last night was
WING-CREDIBLE!
Humbleton's family gave
us pony rides to the
Old Oak Tree.

This is
flaperrific!

66

Then we all took turns saying the Owl Oath. Finally, it was my turn.

First, I'd just like to thank everyone for getting me here. I want to say a special thank-you to my new friend Humbleton. He taught me that sometimes being <u>wise</u> doesn't mean being right. It can mean being able to see where you went wrong and to learn from it. He also taught me that being <u>brave</u> doesn't mean never being scared. It means trying to do what's right, even when you do feel scared.

I took a deep breath and said the oath.

We are owls,
brave and true.
We help each other
and others, too.
We're wise and kind,
through and through!
We are owls!
Too-wit! Too-woo!

All the animals cheered.
Well done, Eva!
You were owlmazing!
I couldn't have done it without you, Humbleton!

We partied all through the night at the **Keepers of the Forest** Ball!

Diary, this was a **FLAP-TASTIC** week! I don't know if I'll always be very brave, wise, and kind. But I learned that as long as I <u>try my hardest</u> to be those things, then that is what counts.

Now I need my sleep. Humbleton is going to take me for a gallop tomorrow!

See you next time!

Rebecca Elliott was a lot like Eva when she was younger: She loved making things and hanging out with her best friends. Now that Rebecca is older, not much has changed — except that her best friends are her husband, Matthew, and their children. She still loves making things, like stories, cakes, music, and paintings. But as much as she and Eva have in common, Rebecca cannot fly or turn her head all the way around. No matter how hard she tries.

Rebecca is the author of JUST BECAUSE and MR. SUPER POOPY PANTS. OWL DIARIES is her first early chapter book series.

OWL DIARIES

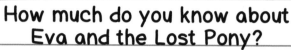

How much do you know about Eva and the Lost Pony?

Why does Eva become a Storm Soldier? In the middle of the story, does Eva think her plan works? What about at the end? Why does her opinion change?

Eva helps Humbleton find his way home. Write about a time when you helped a friend.

Eva's posters give tips on how to stay safe in a storm. What are some ways you stay safe in bad weather? Create your own poster of storm-safety tips.

Why do Eva's parents have a talk with her when she comes home after the storm? Reread page 46.

The Owl Oath is all about helping others. Work with a partner to come up with creative ways you can show kindness to your classmates or help out in your community. Turn back to pages 50–53 for inspiration!